Usborne
A Sticker Dolly Story
Dolphin Magic

Zanna Davidson

Illustrated by Heather Burns
Cover illustration by Antonia Miller

Use the stickers to dress the Dolls on the 'Meet the Dolls' pages

Meet the Dolphin Rescue Dolls

This is the first time Jack, Holly and Olivia have worked together as a team. They all share a passion for animals and protecting wildlife. Together, they are the 'Dolphin Rescue Dolls'.

Jack

is an Animal Rescue Doll. He has a passion for sea creatures. He is also a keen birdwatcher and is never without his binoculars.

Use the stickers to dress the Dolls

Holly

is a Magic Doll. She has a special relationship with trees and woodland creatures. She also loves the mermaids that live on the Enchanted Isle.

Olivia

is a Princess Doll. She spends as much time as she can outside. She loves plants and animals and is an excellent horse rider.

Dolly Town

The Dolphin Rescue Dolls all live in Dolly Town, where Dolls work in teams to help those in trouble. They are the very best at what they do, whether that's animal rescue, magical missions or caring for nature. Each day brings with it an exciting new adventure…

The **Shooting Star** train whisks the Dolls away on their missions.

The Dolls love to celebrate at the **Cupcake Café.**

Madame Coco's **Costume Emporium** has everything the Dolls might need.

Rose Theatre

The **Animal Sanctuary** is where the Animal Rescue Dolls work.

Bluebell Bookshop

Evergreen Sports Arena

Royal Palace is home to the Princess Dolls.

Heartbeat Dance Academy

Palm Tree Film Studios

Fashion Design Studio

Mission Control Centre lets the Dolls know who's in trouble and where to go.

Pop Star Stadium

Silver Sparkles Skating Rink

Strawberry Lane Stables

Honeysuckle Cottage is home to the Magic Dolls.

DOLLY TOWN SUMMER PARTY

Chapter One

Party at the Palace

The Princess Dolls, Meera, Sophia and Olivia, were full of nervous excitement. It was Midsummer's Day and they were getting ready to host a garden party at the palace.

From the balcony, they could see the very first of the guests arriving.

The guests were making their way down the drive to the elegant marquee on the palace lawn.

"At last!" said Meera. "It's time for the party to begin. Shall we go down and greet everyone?"

"Let's," agreed Olivia. And together they made their way down the sweeping palace staircase and out into the sunny gardens.

They stood by the marquee's entrance to greet the guests. There were the Magic Dolls, the Animal Rescue Dolls, the Nature Dolls…

and, of course, Madame Coco, in a
stunning chiffon dress.

"Everything looks perfect," said
Madame Coco, smiling at them.

"You must have spent so long preparing for today."

Sophia looked over at the bouquets of flowers on the tables, the splashing fountains and happy, laughing guests, and knew that all the hard work had been worth it.

While the Princess Dolls greeted everyone, waiters brought round trays of delicious canapés and

sparkling fruit cocktails in crystal glasses. But just as the Princess Dolls were welcoming the last of the guests, their mission watches began to flash.

Olivia quickly tapped her screen and Meera and Sophia gathered round.

"We have an emergency situation," said Mission Control, "and a rather *unusual* mission."

"Go on," said Meera.

"We know it's your Summer Party," Mission Control went on, "but we're going to need a Princess Doll, a Magic Doll and an Animal Rescue Doll."

"Goodness!" said Meera. "This must be a very special case. I'll let everyone know."

She climbed onto one of the chairs and rang a bell to attract everyone's attention.

"We've had a message from Mission Control," Meera announced.

"They've asked for a Magic Doll, a Princess Doll and an Animal Rescue Doll for a rather unusual mission. Would anyone like to volunteer?"

At once, the marquee broke into excited murmurs as everyone wondered what the mysterious mission could be.

Two hands went up immediately
– Holly, one of the Magic Dolls
and Jack, one of the Animal
Rescue Dolls.

"Thank you!" said Meera, and
she beckoned Holly and Jack over
to the marquee entrance, where
Olivia was waiting.

"They need a Princess Doll as

well," said Olivia, "and I think I should be the one to go. You and Sophia have worked so hard preparing for the party. You deserve to enjoy it. And if they want an Animal Rescue Doll, it sounds as though animals will be involved, and that's definitely *my* kind of mission."

"Are you sure?" asked Meera.

"I'm sure," said Olivia. "I'll tell you all about the mission when I get back. Have fun at the party!"

"Good luck!" said Meera.

Olivia turned to Holly and Jack. "Let's go to the palace conservatory," she said. "It'll be quiet there, and a good place to find out more about the mission."

When they reached the conservatory, Jack gazed in delight at the sweet-scented orange trees and the little iridescent hummingbirds flitting from flower to flower.

"Ready?" said Olivia. The others nodded.

Olivia tapped her watch. "Come in, Mission Control," she said.

The team is ready. What's the mission?

Sorry to take you away from the Summer Party, but we have an EMERGENCY. We've had a call from Princess Callista on Coral Island. The princess has noticed a dolphin mother and her baby trapped in a bay – they're circling around and can't get out again. They seem lost and confused. The princess' parents are preparing for an important visit and she didn't know who else to ask for help.

All three Dolls exchanged glances and nodded. "Of course we'll help," said Holly.

"Thank you," said Mission Control. "We needed a Princess Doll as it's happening in royal waters, and an Animal Rescue Doll to help with the dolphin rescue. We asked for a Magic Doll, too, in case you need to ask the mermaids for help. I know you've never worked together before," Mission Control went on, "but you'll make the perfect team. We'll send through the mission details now..."

Dolphin Rescue

Mission details:

Rescue the mother dolphin and her baby from the shallow bay on Coral Island.

The baby is just a few weeks old and is keeping close to its mother's side.

Check for injuries or ill health, and be ready to call upon the mermaids if you need extra help.

THE DOLPHINS

The mother and baby are striped dolphins.
These dolphins are very acrobatic and live in
large groups. Dolphin babies are known as calves.

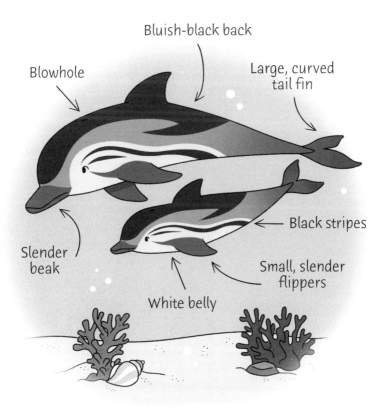

Bluish-black back

Blowhole

Large, curved
tail fin

Black stripes

Slender
beak

Small, slender
flippers

White belly

CALLISTA THE CORAL PRINCESS

Blue eyes

Long, wavy
dark hair

Cotton top
with scalloped
neckline

Flared shorts
with a frilled
hem

Gold woven
sandals

"The princess will be waiting for you at her Summer Palace, which overlooks the bay," said Mission Control. "You'll also need royal permission to enter the water."

"We'll leave right away," said Jack.

"Sienna has already left the party to ready the Shooting Star train," said Mission Control. "And Madame Coco is preparing your outfits."

"Thank you," said Olivia. "Madame Coco's, here we come!"

Chapter Two

Madame Coco at the Ready

Holly, Jack and Olivia quickly left the palace. Olivia smiled to hear the excited chatter of the guests wafting down the drive as they made their way to Madame Coco's, but her mind was now fixed firmly on the mission ahead.

They crossed Dolly Town under

a cloudless sky, the sun beaming down. Then they stepped through the revolving door into the cool quiet of the department store and headed straight for the glass elevator.

"Good day," said Jasper, the lift attendant, and the Dolls saw that he, too, was still in his party clothes.

Madame Coco asked me to take you to Floor Number 3.

Once the Dolls were inside, Jasper pressed the button and the lift whizzed up and up before coming to a stop with a gentle

TING!

Then the Dolls stepped out into the Animal Rescue Department.

Madame Coco was already there, eagerly waiting to greet them.

"We're so sorry you had to leave the party," said Olivia.

"This is much more important," said Madame Coco, with a graceful wave of her hand. "There will be other parties, but this is a *mission*. Now," she went on, looking serious, "I've received the details and I have your outfits ready – everything you could need to help you rescue those poor dolphins."

Holly's clothes

Pretty pink flower
hair decoration

Floral pink
and green
wetsuit

Purple aqua
shoes

Jack's clothes

Striped blue
t-shirt

Palm print
swim shorts

Green and blue
aqua shoes

Olivia's clothes

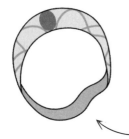

Hair scarf

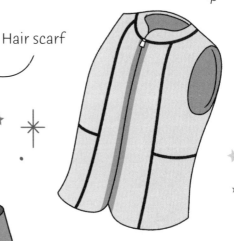

Teal rash vest
with pink zip

Leaf print
swim leggings

Teal and pink
aqua shoes

"I've also put together a dolphin rescue kit," Madame Coco went on, "and a support stretcher, in case you need to lift the dolphins.

Now follow me to Floor 6 everyone. We need to pay a little visit to the Royal Department Floor…"

The Dolls stepped inside the lift again, Jasper pressed the button and this time they arrived at a large room lined with plush red carpet, full of ballgowns and glittering jewels.

"Wow!" said Holly, taking it all in. "What beautiful dresses."

"But I'm not sure we'll be needing any of this today!" said Jack, looking around.

"When you're visiting a royal isle," insisted Madame Coco, "you always need to be prepared.

Now, Olivia, I've packed a little bag, so should the occasion arise, you can all three present yourself to the King and Queen of Coral Island."

"Thank you, Madame Coco," said Olivia, smiling as she took the bag.

"One final floor to visit," said Madame Coco, summoning them back to the lift. "Floor number 7 please, Jasper. The Magical Department Floor."

"Oh!" said Olivia. "I've never been here before. How exciting!"

This room felt very different to the others. It was small, but airy, and felt somehow as if it were filled with the soft green light of a forest.

"For you, Holly," said Madame Coco. "Some magic calming dust, to help soothe the dolphins if they feel worried. And…" she went on, "this very special skirt."

"Wow!" said Holly.

"When this skirt touches the water," Madame Coco explained,

"you'll be able to sense all the life around you – from jellyfish and sharks to friendly porpoises. It will help keep you, and the dolphins, safe from danger."

"Oh! Thank you," said Holly, taking the skirt and the little sparkling bag. "And I'm wearing my necklace too," Holly went on, touching the row of pearly shells around her neck, "so I can call on the mermaids if I need them."

Then the Dolls saw their names flashing up above the changing rooms.

When they stepped out again,
they were dressed and ready for
their mission.

Back outside, on the
sunny street, Sienna was waiting
for them in the Shooting Star train.

"Well, it's not often I wear a
dress to drive my train!" she said,
smiling down at her party outfit.
"Where do I need to take you on
your mission?"

MISSION LOCATION:

Coral Island

Old Town

Coral Reefs

Far Mountains of the
Enchanted Isle

Summer Palace

The Coral Princess
will be waiting for
you here

Cowrie
Caves

Coral Bay

"Step aboard," said Sienna. "I'll have you there in no time."

As the train doors swished shut behind them, Olivia, Jack and Holly all looked at each other, smiling shyly.

"I know we've never worked as a team before," said Olivia, "but I'm sure that, together, we can save the dolphins."

"I think it would help if we gave ourselves a name," suggested Jack. "How about the Dolphin Rescue Dolls?"

"Brilliant!" said Olivia.

"I like it too," said Holly. "And now," she added, as the train began to move…

It's Mission Go!

Chapter Three
Dolphin in Danger

T he Shooting Star train wound its way through Dolly Town and entered a dark tunnel, sparkling with stars.

With a

WHOOSH

the train shot out the other side.

The Dolls peered out of the windows to see they were crossing the Majestic Isle, skimming through the wildflower glades of the Woodland Kingdom, and then out across a glittering sea.

At last, they reached a tiny island ringed by beautiful coral reefs, and came to stop on a white sandy beach, tucked away in a little bay.

Above them, rising up with pale pink turrets and jutting balconies, was the Summer Palace.

"Here you are," said Sienna, drawing to a halt beside the palace. "And it looks like Princess Callista is waiting for you on the balcony."

"Thank you!" said Holly as, one by one, the Dolls stepped off the train and made their way up the marble steps towards the palace balcony.

"Oh, I'm so glad you're here,"
said Princess Callista, hurrying over
to meet them. "Come this way,"
she went on, leading them to a
shady corner.

As they followed Callista, Olivia
noticed how the princess kept
looking this way and that, as if to
make sure no one had seen them.
Only when they were huddled
under a giant fern, hidden from
view, did she start speaking.

"I'm hoping you can help save
the dolphins," she began. "I have

a horrible feeling they're stuck in the bay."

"Could you tell us everything you know about them?" asked Jack.

The princess nodded. "I was down on the beach this morning," she said, "and I saw a striped dolphin mother and her calf swimming in the bay. I could see the rest of the pod, too, leaping and jumping out of the water, but they were much further out. It looked as

if they were trying to call to the mother to join them again."

Callista stopped speaking as she heard a rustling in the branches, but carried on as a little lizard peeped through the leaves.

"The mother and her calf stayed in the bay. I kept watching them as

they don't usually
come this close, and
it seems to me they're
getting closer and
closer to the shore.
The water's so
shallow I'm really
worried that they'll
get stuck! My
parents, the King
and Queen of

Coral Island, have been busy all morning, preparing for a royal visit, and I didn't know who else to turn to…"

"You did the right thing," said Olivia. "Now, we'd better get down to the water to see what's going on."

"Yes, do hurry!" said Princess Callista, and it seemed to Olivia that she was trying to usher them away from the palace as quickly as possible.

But just as they reached the steps, the palace doors burst open and the King and Queen stepped onto the balcony.

Princess Callista turned to look at them, a horror-struck expression on her face.

"Callista," said the King. "You haven't made a fuss about those dolphins, have you?"

He looked over at the Dolphin Rescue Dolls. "Because if that's what you're here for, I'm going to have to stop you! No one, and I mean *no one*, is allowed to set foot in our waters!"

Chapter Four

Royal Waters

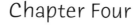

Holly and Jack both let out a gasp, as if they couldn't believe what the King had just told them. Then they turned to Olivia, hoping she would know how to deal with the situation.

Olivia took a deep breath. "Your Majesty," she began, keeping her voice polite. "What seems to be the problem?"

"The problem," huffed the King, "as my daughter, Callista, very well knows, is that we have a HUGELY important meeting at the palace today with the Empress of Turtle Island. For many years our islands have been on extremely unfriendly terms.

The Empress is coming on a mission of peace and we need to show her how welcome she is. Everything must look PERFECT."

"Indeed," added the Queen. "We've arranged for a performance on the beach, with musicians and entertainers. We can't have you splashing about with dolphins in the background."

"But, Your Majesty," Olivia replied, "if we don't go and rescue the dolphins, they could die!"

The King held up his hand. "Really?" he said. "I'm sure the dolphins will be fine until this evening. You can come back and look at them then. Dolphins are sea creatures, after all, and they're *in* the sea. But for now, I must insist you leave so we can get everything ready for the Empress. May I remind you that you need my permission to enter royal waters – and I'm *not* going to give it to you."

Jack and Holly began to look

really worried, but Olivia refused
to give up.

"I'm afraid the dolphins aren't
going to be okay if we leave them,"
she said, quietly but firmly. "The
chances are, the mother and her
calf will become even more anxious

and confused and become stranded on the beach. If that happens, you'll have a couple of dolphins stuck on your beach. How will *that* look to the Empress of Turtle Island?"

At this, the Queen furrowed her brow and looked questioningly at the King. "She does make a good point…"

"What's more," Olivia went on, "I'm sure the Empress will be all the *more* impressed with you, if you tell her we're here to save sea creatures that have become stranded in royal waters. I'm sure she'd want to know you care for all the animals that live on your island."

"Well…" blustered the King, "I suppose you can at least *try* to sort out these dolphins now."

"Yes," agreed the Queen. "You have permission to enter our waters for exactly one hour. But you'll need to have the dolphins back out to sea by then, for that is when the Empress is due to arrive! We don't want the beach littered with all your messy equipment."

The Dolls exchanged relieved glances. "Thank you, Your Majesty. We'll get to it right away," said Olivia.

"Can I come too?" asked Callista.

Olivia looked at the King and Queen.

"Yes, you may," replied the King. "But I want you back here, clean *and* dry, as soon as the Empress arrives."

"Thank you," said Callista. She turned to the Dolls. "Follow me," she said. "I'll take you to where I last saw the dolphins."

Without a moment's delay, the Dolls followed Callista as she rushed down towards the bay. When she reached the beach, she pointed, and there, not far from the shore, they could make out the dolphin mother and her calf.

Jack immediately reached for his binoculars for a closer look. "Well, the good news is that I can't see any injuries," he said. "They both look a good colour and seem healthy. But the bad news is that the dolphin mother really is stuck."

"Oh no!" cried Callista.

"I don't know why she's come into such shallow waters," said Jack, "but now she's lying on her side in

the sand. Part of her body's above the water, which means she could easily get sunburnt. The baby won't leave her side, so I'm afraid he's in danger of getting stuck as well."

"What shall we do?" asked Holly.

"We'll need to approach the dolphin and see if we can dig out

the sand from underneath her – and
then get her floating again. That will
be the least stressful thing for her."
Jack turned to the others. "We'll
have to walk out to the dolphins,
which means entering the water.
Are you all okay with that?"

Everyone nodded.

"May I come too?" asked Princess
Callista, a pleading note in her voice.

"I appreciate your help," said
Jack, "but too many people will only

make the dolphins even more
anxious. Would you stay here while
we investigate? Then if we need
the stretcher, you could bring it
out to us."

Callista nodded. "Of course,"
she said.

Jack, Olivia and Holly began
walking through the shallow waters
towards the dolphins, trying not to
think about how little time they
had before the Empress arrived.

As the first, gentle waves lapped at Holly's skirt, she let out a gasp. At once, she could feel the magic working, just as Madame Coco had said. She began to have an incredible sense of all the life around her – the little fish darting around the coral, the jellyfish floating near the sunlit surface, and the dolphins, too, stressed and anxious, just across from them in the shallows.

"These waters are safe," she told the others...

And the closer they came, the more they could see the mother dolphin's panic. She started thrashing from side to side on the sand. Her little calf was keeping his distance, unsure of the Dolls, but

reluctant to leave his mother.

"Oh no," said Jack. "The mother's body is starting to tilt nearer the water. If her blowhole goes under the surface, then she could drown. We're going to have to move fast to save her!"

Chapter Five
Out to Sea

"What do we need to do first?" asked Holly, as they reached the dolphin's side.

"Keep away from her tail," Jack said. "It's very powerful. Avoid her beak, too," he added. "A panicked dolphin might bite, as she may not realize we're here to help her."

Holly nodded. Keeping her movements slow and gentle, she began to sprinkle some of Madame Coco's magic calming dust over the dolphin. It sparkled as it fell through the air, then settled over the dolphin's gleaming back.

After just a few moments, she
seemed to become less panicked
and her breathing grew steadier.

Meanwhile, Jack had started pulling
out some cloths from the rescue kit
and handed them to the others.
"Dip these in seawater," he said,

"and then lay them over the dolphin. Be careful not to cover her fin or blowhole," he added. "It will help to stop her from getting sunburnt."

As soon as the dolphin was covered, Jack asked them to begin digging. "We need to remove the sand from under her body. Hopefully we'll be able to free her so she can swim away on her own."

As they worked, Jack tried to keep an eye on the baby dolphin, which was still swimming in the waters just beyond his mother.

"I'm not sure this is working," said Olivia, breathless from all the digging. "As soon as we dig away the sand, it fills up again!"

"And the mother is looking more and more distressed," added Holly.

"You're right," said Jack. "This is getting urgent. We're going to need the stretcher. It will be more stressful for the dolphin, but we don't have a choice."

He waved over to Callista. "Could you bring the stretcher please?" he called.

Princess Callista nodded and quickly made her way through the shallow water.

"Thank you," said Jack. "Let's each take a corner of the stretcher. Then we need to slide it under the dolphin's body. But first, Holly, can you give the baby some of your magic calming dust? I don't want him to take fright and swim away."

Holly sprinkled the last of the magic dust over the little calf. "It's going to be okay," she said, keeping her voice gentle and calm.

Then she grasped her corner
of the stretcher and they began to
ease it, slowly and carefully, under
the dolphin mother.

"That's great," said Jack, with a
brief smile. "And now, we need to

carry her out to the deeper water."

Everyone nodded, and on the count of three, they lifted the dolphin and began walking with her through the water, away from the shore.

"Well done," said Holly, whispering to the dolphin. "You're doing well. We're nearly there."

"Isn't she beautiful?" added Olivia. "I've never seen a dolphin this close before. I can't get over the intelligence in her eyes."

As they walked further out to sea, Holly was aware of the little calf swimming behind them, but always keeping his distance.

When they were nearly waist high, Jack gave another nod. "This'll do," he said. "We're deep enough now."

With his free hand, he removed the wet cloths from the dolphin and placed them over his shoulder.

"On the count of three," he said, "let's slowly remove the stretcher from under the dolphin's body…"

Jack counted and on 'three', they began to pull away the stretcher…

"Oh! Hooray!" whispered Holly. "Look at that! She's swimming again!"

"And there's her calf, following in her wake," said Jack, grinning. "We've done it! Thank goodness we've done it."

"And just in time, too!" said Olivia, checking her watch. "The Empress will be here soon!"

They turned and began walking back up towards the beach, Princess Callista skipping with excitement. "I can't believe I just helped to rescue a dolphin," she said. "What could be more magical than that!"

"I'll just do a final check," said Jack, picking up his binoculars once they reached the shore. "Oh no!" he exclaimed, gazing through them.

"What's the matter?" asked Holly. "What is it?"

"It's the dolphin mother and her baby," said Jack. "They're coming back! They're headed into shore again!"

Chapter Six

Mermaid Magic

E veryone could see now that
Jack was right. The dolphins
were clearly headed
back into the bay.

"What are we going to do?" gasped Callista.

"It's almost as if the dolphins are trying to tell us something," said Olivia. "But what?"

She glanced over at Holly. "Do you think they're trying to escape danger?"

But Holly shook her head. "I didn't sense anything," she said. "I don't think there's anything *in* the water that's scaring them."

Jack's brow was creased with worry. "If they keep heading this way, the dolphin mother is going to get stuck again. And even if we free her, she may well just keep returning. We *have* to work out what's wrong!"

"And what's more," added Callista, "the Empress will be here soon and my parents will ask you to leave. I'm not sure I'm going to be able to persuade them to change their minds…"

"I think it's time for some magic," said Holly, reaching for her shell necklace. "I'll call on the mermaids. The Enchanted Isle isn't far from here, and the mermaids have always said I can call on them when needed."

"Oh!" said Princess Callista, excitedly. "I've heard of the mermaids before but I've never seen one."

"They're very shy," explained Holly. "I do hope they answer…"

She reached
for her shell
necklace and
began to blow over
the row of tiny shells.
At once they began to
glow and a faint sparkle filled
the air. They all looked out to sea,
desperately hoping to catch a
glimpse of a mermaid. But there was
nothing to see beyond the mother
dolphin and her calf, coming ever
closer into the shallows.

"Please answer…"
murmured Holly.

Then came a gentle
humming, followed by a song
that sounded as if it was made
from foam and wind and sky.

"I recognize that sound!"
said Holly, joyfully, and a
moment later a mermaid
rose up out of the waves.

"Oh, Nerissa!" called Holly, her voice full of relief as she recognized her mermaid friend.

Nerissa smiled back and Holly quickly explained about the dolphin and her baby and how they were trying to help them.

"Do you have a way of communicating with dolphins?" asked Holly. "We need to know why they keep coming back into the bay."

Nerissa nodded and dived beneath the surface. They could

just make out her tail, undulating through the water, and then she appeared again, just a little distance from the dolphins.

She spoke to them in their language, and the dolphin mother replied in a series of squeaks and whistles.

Nerissa nodded and then turned to Holly. "The dolphin mother is worried about her baby," she explained. "She says she needs your help."

Her baby is in trouble.

"May I take a look?" asked Jack. He walked over to the baby dolphin and this time the little calf didn't swim away but stayed still, letting Jack look him over.

"Oh! She's right!" cried Jack.
"How could I have missed this?
I was so focused on the mother
that I didn't see… The poor baby
has some fishing twine wrapped
around his flipper. It's transparent
so it's hard to spot, but it's
definitely there. It must be
cutting into him."

Jack leaned over and slowly
began to unwind the twine from
around the little dolphin's flipper.
The mother dolphin stayed
close while Nerissa placed her
hand on the little dolphin, and

made soothing noises which
seemed to calm him, as if he
knew they were helping him.

When the last piece of twine
had come away, Jack carefully
inspected the flipper.

"There's no wound," he said, his voice filled with relief. "But I'm so glad we were able to remove it. If the twine had stayed, it would have got tighter as the dolphin grew, and that would have been very dangerous for him. He'll be much more comfortable now."

Jack stepped back from the calf, and both mother and baby opened their mouths and let out a series of long, fluting whistles.

"They're saying *thank you!*" said Nerissa.

Jack grinned. "We're just glad we could help."

He reached out and gently touched the dolphins.

The others smiled and waved as the dolphins turned and swam out to sea. When they reached the edge of the bay, they jumped out of the water together in a series of dazzling, graceful leaps.

"Wow!" said Olivia. "Just look at that. One happy mother and baby. What an incredible experience."

"Thank you, Nerissa," said Holly. "We couldn't have done it without you."

"I'll always be there when you need me, Holly," Nerissa replied.

Then, with a final wave, she dived beneath the surface. For a moment her shimmering tail was visible above the water, and then she disappeared from view.

"I can't believe I met a mermaid," said Princess Callista, clapping her hands together in excitement. "*And* we were able to save the dolphins."

"I know," said Olivia, smiling at her. "I'll never forget this."

Together, they walked back up the beach, only to see the King and Queen waiting for them on the palace balcony. The King gestured to them to come up.

"Oh dear," said Olivia. "We must have taken too long…"

When they reached the top step, dripping water along the way, the Dolls saw that the Empress had already arrived. She was surrounded by courtiers and looked incredibly grand, with a long, satin gown and glittering emerald tiara.

"Your Majesty," said Princess
Callista, curtseying before her.

Olivia and Holly did the same while Jack made a low bow.

The Empress smiled at Callista and then turned to the Dolls.

The King tells me you came here on a mission to rescue two dolphins in the bay.

"Yes," replied Olivia. "The mother dolphin was seeking help for her calf. He had some twine wrapped around his flipper. Luckily, we were able to set him free."

"What an incredible mission," said the Empress. "My island is called Turtle Island because of

all the turtles that come to nest there – and nothing is more important to us than guarding their precious eggs and hatchlings.

It's lovely to see Coral Island caring for its wildlife too."

"Yes, *yes*," said the King, quickly. "The wildlife here is *very* important to us."

Olivia looked at him, raising an eyebrow, and the King had the grace to blush.

"Thank you for calling on us,"
Olivia said to Callista. "And let us
know if you ever need our
help again."

"Oh, you're not leaving already,
are you?" said the Empress.

"Yes, do stay for tea," added the
Queen. "It's the least we can do for
you after, well…we may not have
been as welcoming as we should have
been when you first arrived."

"I'm afraid we're not really dressed
for the occasion," laughed Holly,
looking down at her wetsuit.

"Oh! Wait a moment!" said Olivia, looking inside the bag that Madame Coco had given her. "I think I might have just the thing! May we use one of your rooms to get changed?"

"Of course," said the Queen. "I'll show you to one now. And Callista, go up to your bedroom. You could do with getting changed too."

The Queen led the Dolls inside the palace, down a cool marble-lined corridor filled with lush plants, to a little side room.

Holly's clothes

Flower hair decoration

Top with leaf detail sleeves

Layered skirt with leaf embroidery

Slip-on sandals

Olivia's clothes

Off-the-shoulder
blouse

Ankle-tie
shoes

Wide leg trousers
with tie belt

Jack's clothes

Smart chino trousers

Short-sleeve patterned shirt

Canvas lace-up shoes

When they stepped out again, a footman led them back to the balcony, where everyone was waiting for them.

By now, a band was playing music on the beach while performers danced across the sand. The Dolls could see the King and Queen really were doing everything they could to impress the Empress.

"Oh, what wonderful clothes!" exclaimed Princess Callista when she saw the Dolls.

"Thank you," said Olivia. "They're from Madame Coco's. She always provides the best outfits!"

Then she turned back to the King and Queen. "We missed our

Summer Party for this mission. So, it would be lovely to stay for tea. Thank you!"

After that, they sat down to a wonderful feast. There were

delectable little dishes – a fragrant coconut broth, exotic salads with avocado and papaya, spicy sweet potatoes – followed by silver bowls of tropical fruit.

Best of all, they
loved hearing
Princess Callista
tell them more
about the dolphins
that lived around the
island, and the Empress' tales of the
rare and beautiful turtles that came
to nest on her beaches.

As the sun set across the island – the sky glowing pink and orange, and the waters of the bay flooded with the same warm colours – the Dolls knew it was time to leave.

Jack tapped his watch to call the Shooting Star train, and they got up to say their goodbyes.

"Do come and visit Turtle Island soon," said the Empress. "I'd love to show you our turtles."

"Thank you," said Olivia, "and thank you for having us for tea," she added, turning to the King and Queen.

Then, with a final wave, the Dolls made their way back to the beach, where Sienna was waiting for them.

"Before you go…" called the King, hurrying down the steps after them, "I wanted to say thank you for all your help today. And to apologise for how I behaved earlier. I was so anxious for the Empress' visit to go perfectly, I forgot what was *really* important – protecting our wildlife. Next time I see a dolphin in trouble, I'll make sure I call on you."

Then the Dolphin Rescue Dolls
stepped aboard the Shooting
Star train.

"Where would you like to go?"
asked Sienna.

Olivia checked her watch.

"The Summer Party will be over now," she said.

"Then let's go to the Cupcake Café!" said Holly. "The perfect place to celebrate our dolphin rescue."

Back in Dolly Town, the Dolphin Rescue Dolls sat together at one of the outdoor tables at the Cupcake Café. Stars were already lighting the evening sky and the café was lit with scented candles and strings of fairy lights.

"I've brought you all ice cream sundaes," said Maya, the café owner. "And to make up for missing the Summer Party, I've added extra sprinkles...and sparklers!"

"Oh, thank you!" said Holly, grinning at her. "I'm glad I left room for pudding!"

"I wouldn't have missed our mission for the world," added Jack.

They all smiled at each other.

"I agree," said Jack.

"Dolphin Rescue Dolls forever," they all chanted together.

The End

Look out for *the*
Animal Rescue Dolls!

Get ready for some new
Sticker Dolly adventures.

Coming soon!

The rescue mission and events in this book are entirely fictional and should never be attempted by anyone other than a trained professional.

Edited by Lesley Sims and Stephanie King
Designed by Hannah Cobley
Additional design by Johanna Furst
Expert advice from Suzanne Rogers

First published in 2022 by Usborne Publishing Ltd.,
Usborne House, 83-85 Saffron Hill, London EC1N 8RT, England.
usborne.com Copyright © 2022 Usborne Publishing Ltd. UKE

All rights reserved. No part of this publication may be reproduced, stored in a retrieval system or transmitted in any form or by any means without the prior permission of the publisher. The name Usborne and the Balloon Logo are Trade Marks of Usborne Publishing Ltd.